ACE VENTURA

WHEN NATURE CALLS ™

PULL-OUT POSTER BOOK

SCHOLASTIC INC.
New York Toronto London Auckland Sydney

ISBN 0-590-74151-9

TM & © 1995 by Morgan Creek Productions, Inc.
All rights reserved. Published by Scholastic Inc.

12 11 10 9 8 7 6 5 4 3 2 1   5 6 7 8 9/9 0/0

Printed in the U.S.A.   08
First Scholastic printing, December 1995

ACE VENTURA
WHEN NATURE CALLS™

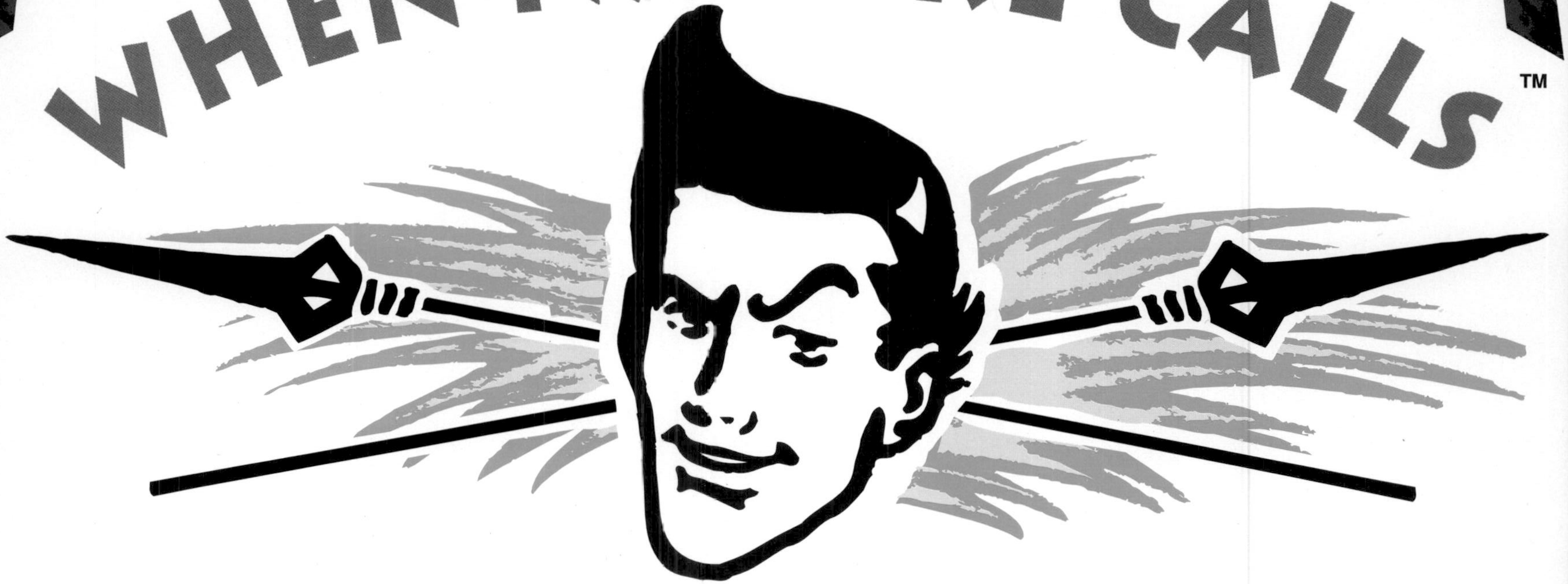

Have you seen a bat? It's like a rat with wings... lifeless beady eyes, clawed feet, huge grotesque wings...

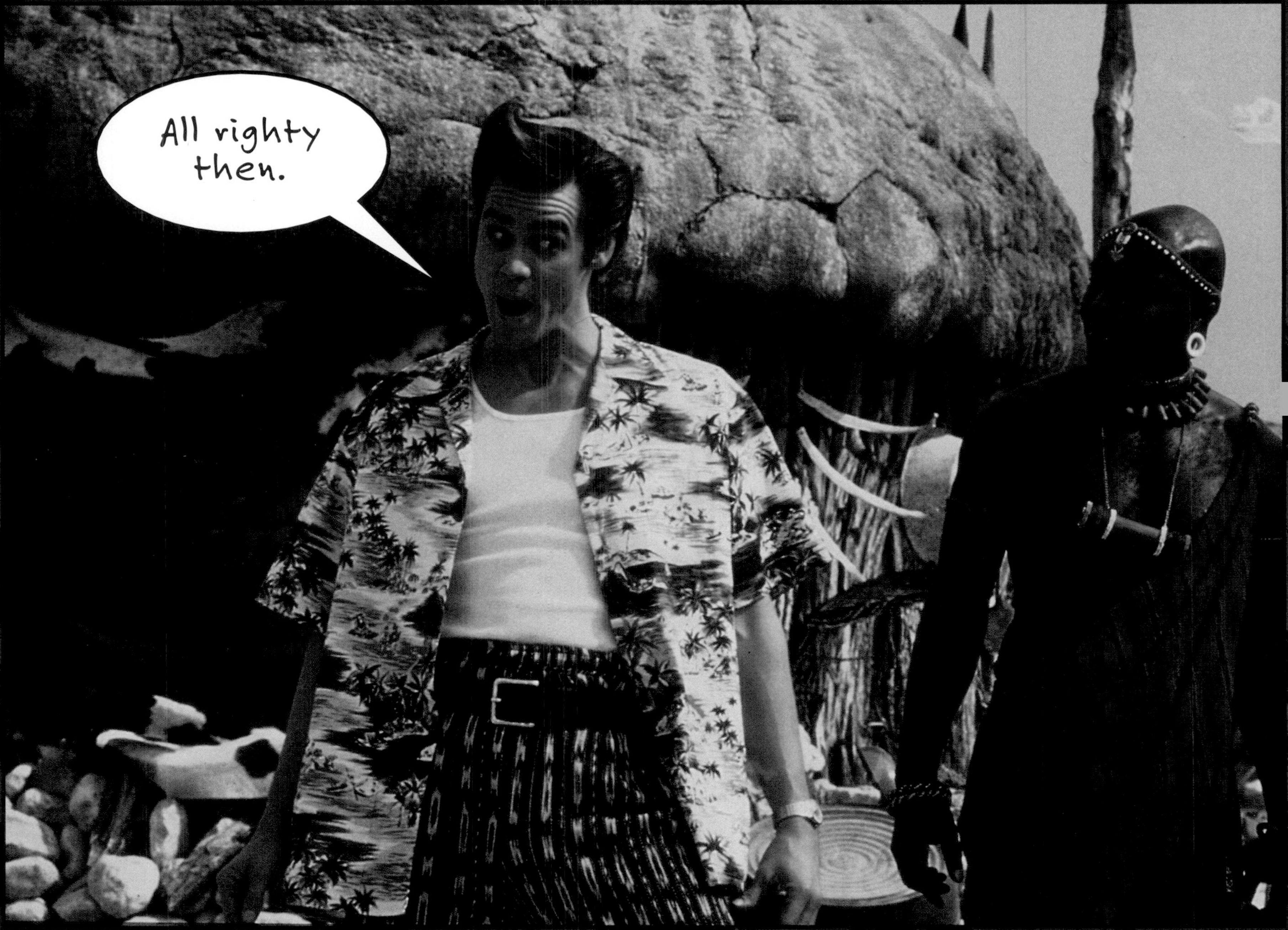
All righty then.

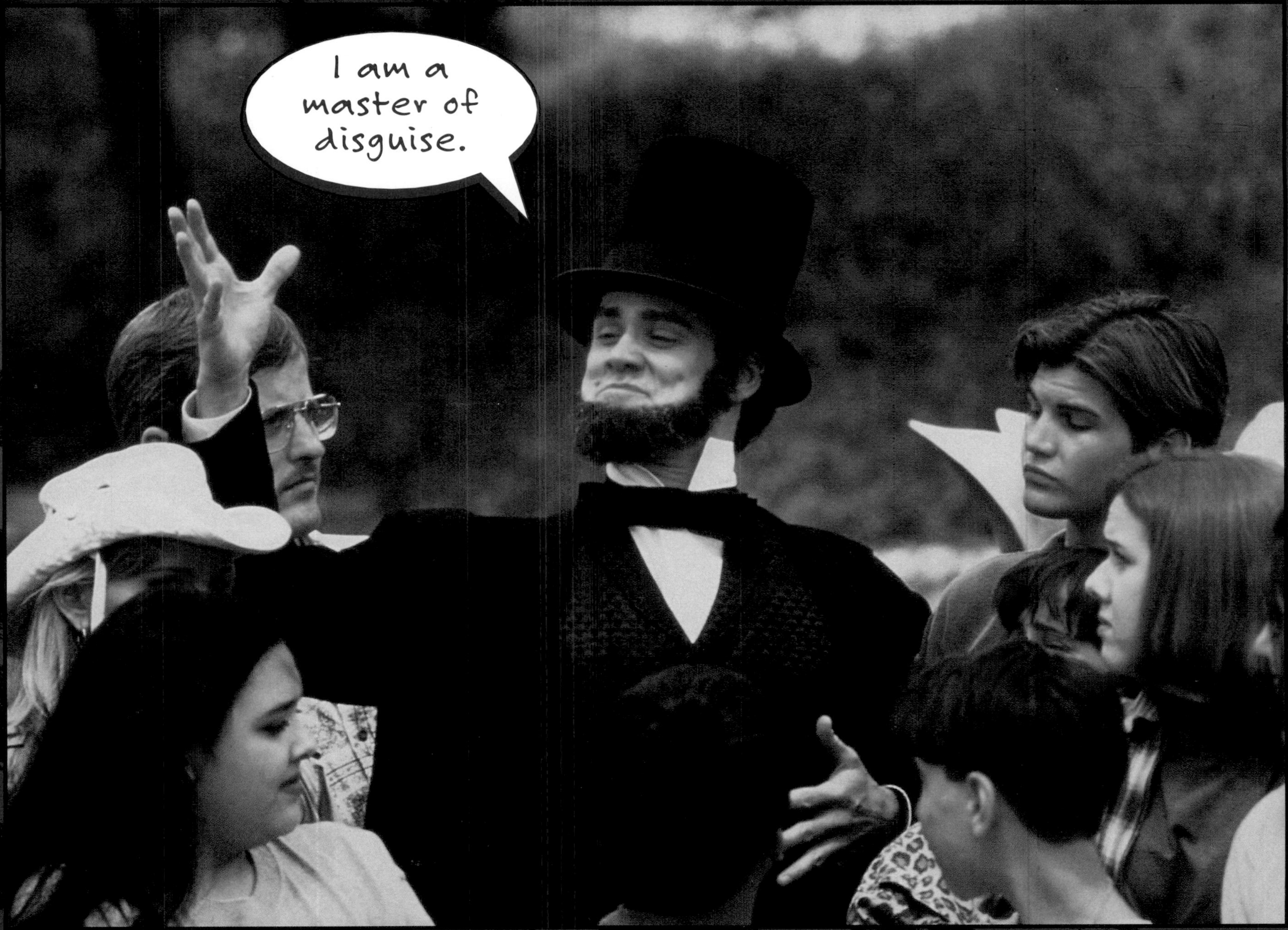
I am a master of disguise.

I'll have you know, I have the reflexes of a cat and the speed of a cheetah.

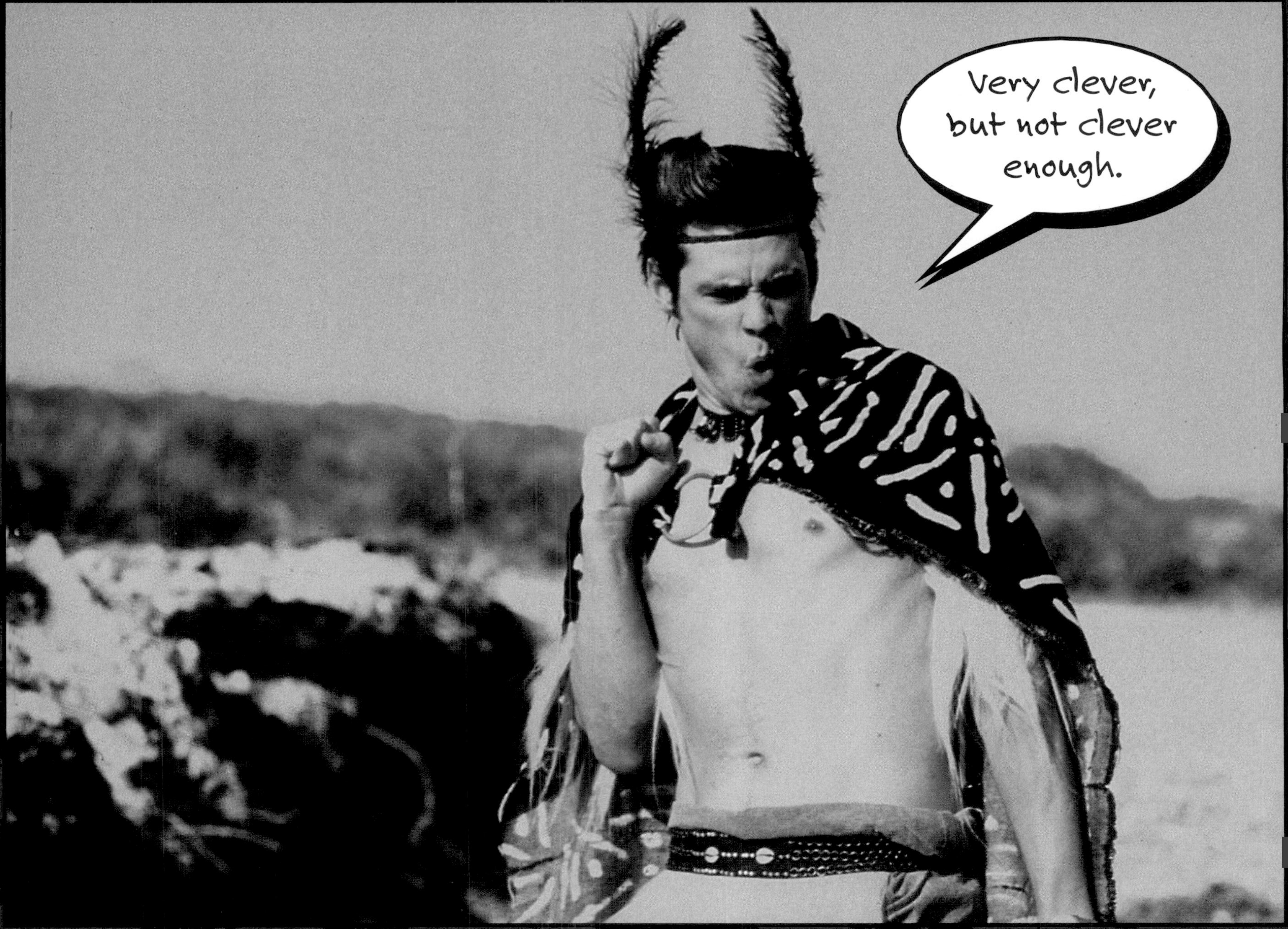
Very clever, but not clever enough.

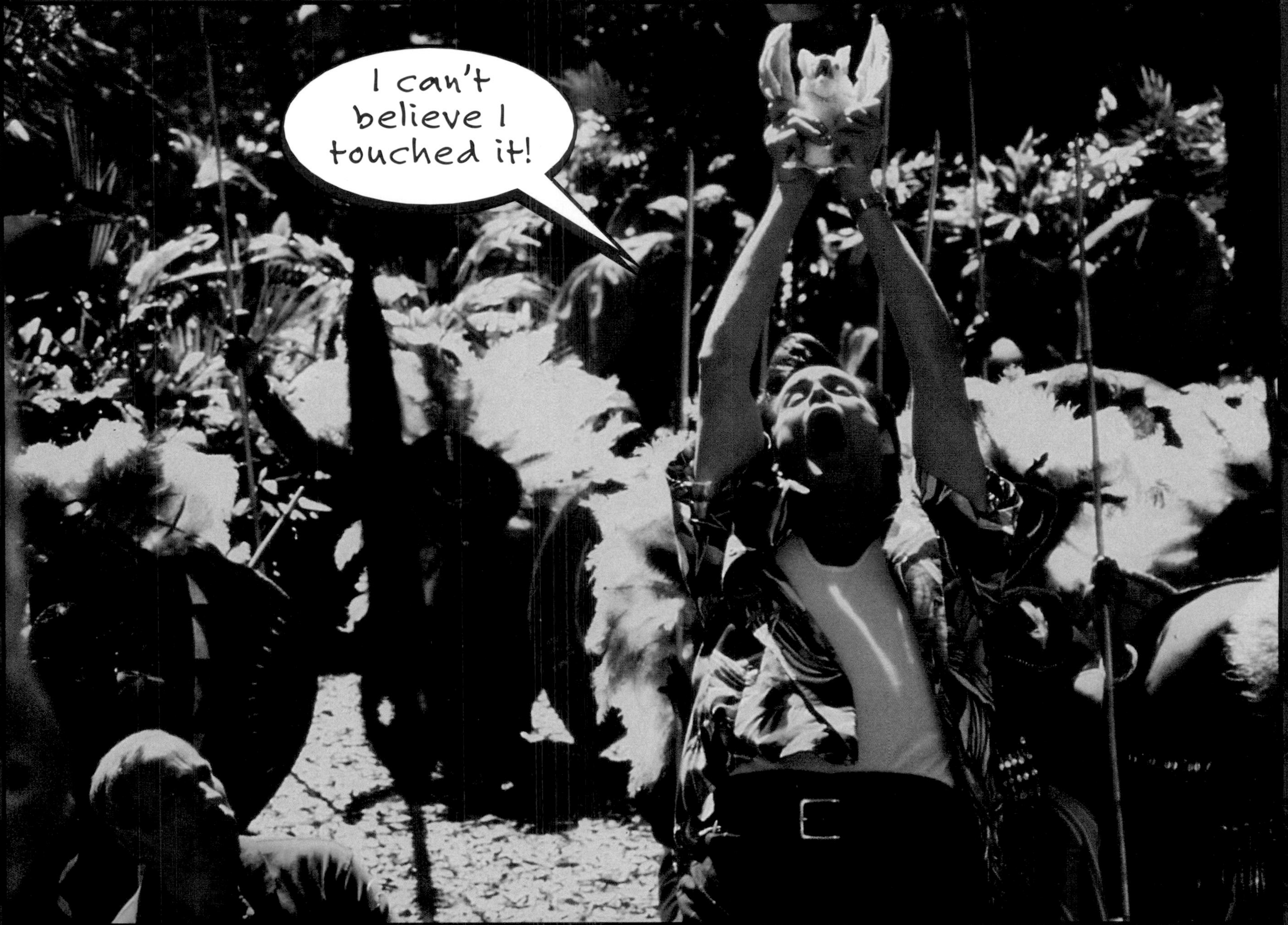
I can't believe I touched it!